I made this
book for:

_____

Love,

Alona

On Grandparents' Farm

Motto:

Vectatio, iterque et mutata
Recio vigorem dabunt

(Travel, turns in the road
and changes of place
add to your strength)

Seneca, Peace of Soul

On Grandparents' Farm

Written and illustrated by

Alona Frankel

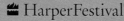
HarperFestival®
A Division of HarperCollinsPublishers

This is Joshua.
Joshua is a little boy.

Once Joshua went for a drive with his mother
and his father, to visit Grandma Scarlett
and Grandpa Emerson Walden.

Grandma Scarlett and Grandpa Emerson Walden
live in the country.

They rode in the old Chevy.
On the road were lots of other cars
carrying lots of other people.

Little cars with big people in them.
Big cars with little people in them.
One was ENORMOUS, as big as a house.
And one car really was a house.

Along the way Joshua saw pine forests
and plowed fields,
fields with amber waves of grain,
and fields jumping with bales of hay;
orchards, vineyards, and gardens;
proud elm trees, flowering vines,
olive groves, and boulevards;
rows of trees lined up on the horizon
like teeth on a comb,

huge sycamores,
and a family picnicking
on a traffic island.

So they drove on and on to visit Grandma Scarlett
and Grandpa Emerson Walden. On the way
Joshua got thirsty and drank from the thermos.
He got hungry and ate something from the cooler.

He had to make wee-wee and made wee-wee
on the side of the road behind the car.
There was a light breeze.
A dry bush scratched his bottom a little
and a pretty partridge flew out, startled,
from the bushes along the road.

They went on driving until suddenly
Joshua smelled freshly harvested
manure. Then he spotted the
tall water tower at the end
of the eucalyptus trees.
And finally, the gate,
the yard, the garden,
the giant mulberry tree,
the red-tile roof,
the small white house.

Grandparents

Garden

Petting Zoo

workshop

DAIRY

BAKERY

HEALTH FOODS

Pool

BED & BREAKFAST

EXIT

And in front Grandma Scarlett
and Grandpa Emerson Walden.
We're here!
What fun!

GARAGE SALE

Everyone was overjoyed.
Grandma Scarlett scuttled around giving hugs and kisses
to Joshua and his mother and father.

Grandpa Emerson Walden patted Joshua's father on the back and said in a very deep voice, "Hello, son."

Then they all sat around the table in the yard, in the shade of the giant mulberry tree, to eat very healthy food: coriander and whole wheat, pickled cauliflower, seeds and nuts, sprigs of mint, soft cheese and olive oil, stuffed carrots and sweet corn. And for dessert: nettle custard pudding.

Nothing was even close to the food Joshua was used to eating at home, except for the corn. Joshua ate the corn.

After lunch,
between two and four o'clock,
everyone went for a nap behind
the closed shutters in the cool house.
Only Grandpa Emerson Walden and Joshua
lay down in the hammock, hanging between
two branches of the giant mulberry tree.
At four in the afternoon,
Joshua went for a walk around the farm
with Grandpa Emerson Walden.

The cow in the cowshed lowed, "Moo-moo-moo-moo!"
The sheep in the sheep pen bleated, "Baa-baa-baa!"

And the goat in the goat pen called "Maa-maa-maa!"
The dove in the dovecot gurgled, "Coo-coo-coo."

The donkey brayed, "Ee-aw! Ee-aw! Ee-aw!"
The horse in the stable whinnied, "Ne-e-e-e-igh!"

And the cat on the roof cried, "Meow-meow-meow!"

The dog in the doghouse barked, "Woof-woof-woof-woof!"
The goose blared, "Honk-honk-honk-honk!"
The chickens in the coop cackled,
"Bawk-bawk-bawk-bawk!"
And the rooster crowed,
"Cock-a-doodle-doo!"

Thousands of flies buzzed, "Bzz-bzz-bzz," and millions of mosquitoes hummed, "Mzz-mzz-mzz-mzz."

They buzzed and they also stung. The fish in the pond were silent.

Joshua and Grandpa Emerson Walden walked back through the vegetable garden. Unpackaged vegetables grew there: plants full of red tomatoes, plants full of green cucumbers, lettuce, cabbage, and cauliflower.

Night fell when they returned. It was time to drive home.
Everyone began to say good-bye.
Grandma Scarlett scuttled around,
kissing Mommy and Daddy and Joshua,
and hugged Joshua real hard.

Grandpa Emerson Walden gave Mommy a kiss, patted Daddy on the back, and said in a very deep voice, "Be seeing you, son." He hugged and kissed Joshua, picked him up and swung him around like a high-speed merry-go-round.

It was a bit sad.
They got into the old Chevy.

They waved good-bye,
blew kisses, and drove off.
Grandma Scarlett and
Grandpa Emerson Walden
stood with their arms
around each other
and waved good-bye.

And what happened on the way back?

Maybe the old Chevy sprouted eagle's wings and flew home?

And maybe an environmentally-friendly giant
carefully picked them up with his gigantic
environmentally-friendly fingers?
Maybe and maybe
and maybe.

But Joshua will never know
because Joshua slept
the whole way home
in the back seat.

Finally, Joshua's mother, Joshua's father, and Joshua arrived home tired, itching, and happy.

What fun!

Grandma Matilda greeted them
with open arms and asked Joshua,
"So, tell me, what does a cow say?"